STORIES
FOR
YOUNG CHILDREN

Illustrated by
Annabel Spenceley

MIMOSA
·BOOKS·

NEW YORK • AVENEL, NEW JERSEY

This edition published in 1993 by Mimosa Books,
distributed by Outlet Book Company, Inc., a Random
House Company, 40 Engelhard Avenue, Avenel,
New Jersey 07001.

2 4 6 8 10 9 7 5 3 1

First published in 1990 by Grisewood & Dempsey Ltd.
Copyright © Grisewood & Dempsey Ltd. 1990

ISBN 1 85698 517 2

Printed and bound in Italy

CONTENTS

THE GINGERBREAD MAN

English Traditional

An old woman was baking one day, and she made some gingerbread. She had some dough left over, so she made the shape of a little man. She made eyes for him, a nose, and a smiling mouth all of currants, and placed more currants down his front to look like buttons. Then she laid him on a baking tray and put him in the oven to bake.

After a little while, she heard something rattling at the oven door. She opened it and to her surprise out jumped the little gingerbread man she had made. She tried to catch him as he ran across the kitchen, but he slipped past her, calling as he ran:

"Run, run, as fast as you can,
You can't catch me, I'm the gingerbread man!"

She chased after him into the garden where her husband was digging. He put down his spade and tried to catch him too, but as the gingerbread man sped past him he called over his shoulder:

"Run, run, as fast as you can,
You can't catch me, I'm the gingerbread man!"

As he ran down the road he passed a cow. The cow called out, "Stop, gingerbread man! You look good to eat!" But the gingerbread man laughed and shouted over his shoulder:

"I've run from an old woman
And an old man.
Run, run, as fast as you can,
You can't catch me, I'm the gingerbread man!"

The cow ran after the old woman and the old man,

and soon they all passed a horse. "Stop!" called out the horse, "I'd like to eat you." But the gingerbread man called out:

"I've run from an old woman
And an old man,
And a cow!
Run, run, as fast as you can,
You can't catch me, I'm the gingerbread man!"

He ran on, with the old woman and the old man and the cow and the horse following, and he went past a party of people haymaking. They all looked up as they saw the gingerbread man, and as he passed them he called out:

"I've run from an old woman,
And from an old man,
And a cow and a horse.
Run, run, as fast as you can,
You can't catch me, I'm the gingerbread man!"

The haymakers joined in the chase behind the old woman and the old man, the cow and the horse, and they all followed him as he ran through the fields. There he met a fox, so he called out to the fox:

"Run, run, as fast as you can,
You can't catch me, I'm the gingerbread man!"

But the sly fox said, "Why should I bother to catch you?" although he thought to himself, "That gingerbread man would be good to eat."

Just after he had run past the fox the gingerbread man had to stop because he came to a wide, deep, swift-flowing river. The fox saw the old woman and the old man, the cow, the horse, and the haymakers all chasing the gingerbread man, so he said.

"Jump on my back, and I'll take you across the river!"

The gingerbread man jumped on the fox's back and

the fox began to swim. As they reached the middle of the river, where the water was deep, the fox said,

"Can you stand on my head, Gingerbread Man, or you will get wet." So the gingerbread man pulled himself up and stood on the fox's head. As the current flowed more swiftly, the fox said,

"Can you move on to my nose, Gingerbread Man, so that I can carry you more safely? I would not like you to drown." The gingerbread man slid onto the fox's nose. But when they reached the bank of the river, the fox suddenly went *snap*! The gingerbread man disappeared into the fox's mouth, and was never seen again.

JACK AND THE BEANSTALK

English Traditional

There was once a boy named Jack who was brave and quick-witted. He lived with his mother in a small cottage and their most valuable possession was their cow, Milky-White. But the day came when Milky-White gave them no milk and Jack's mother said she must be sold.

"Take her to market," she told Jack, "and mind you get a good price for her."

So Jack set out to market leading Milky-White by her halter. After a while he sat down to rest by the side of the road. An old man came by and Jack told him where he was going.

"Don't bother to go to the market," the old man said. "Sell your cow to me. I will pay you well. Look at these beans. Only plant them, and overnight you will find you have the finest bean plants in all the world. You'll be better off with these beans than with an old cow or money. Now, how many is five, Jack?"

"Two in each hand and one in your mouth," replied Jack, as sharp as a needle.

"Right you are, here are five beans," said the old man and he handed the beans to Jack and took Milky-White's halter.

When Jack reached home, his mother said, "Back so soon, Jack? Did you get a good price for Milky-White?"

Jack told her how he had exchanged the cow for five beans and before he could finish his account, his mother started to shout and box his ears. "You lazy good-for-nothing boy!" she screamed, "How could you hand over

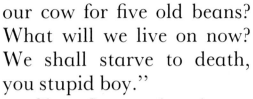

our cow for five old beans? What will we live on now? We shall starve to death, you stupid boy."

She flung the beans through the open window and sent Jack to bed without his supper.

When Jack woke the next morning there was a strange green light in his room. All he could see from the window was green leaves. A huge beanstalk had shot up overnight. It grew higher than he could see. Quickly Jack got dressed and stepped out of the window right onto the beanstalk and started to climb.

"The old man said the beans would grow overnight," he thought. "They must indeed be very special beans."

Higher and higher Jack climbed until at last he reached the top and found himself on a strange road. Jack followed it until he came to a great castle where he could smell the most delicious breakfast. Jack was hungry. It had been a long climb and he had had nothing to eat since midday the day before. Just as he reached the door of the castle he nearly tripped over the feet of an enormous woman.

"Here, boy," she called. "What are you doing? Don't you know my husband likes to eat boys for breakfast? It's lucky I have already fried up some bacon and mushrooms for him today, or I'd pop you in the frying pan. He can eat you tomorrow, though."

"Oh, please don't let him eat me," pleaded Jack. "I only came to ask you for a bite to eat. It smells so delicious."

Now the giant's wife had a kind heart and did not really enjoy cooking boys for breakfast, so she gave Jack a bacon sandwich. He was still eating it when the ground began to shake with heavy footsteps, and a loud voice boomed: "Fee, Fi, Fo, Fum."

"Quick, hide!" cried the giant's wife and she pushed Jack into the oven. "After breakfast, he'll fall asleep," she whispered. "That is when you must creep away." She left the oven door open a crack so that Jack could see into the room. Again the terrible rumbling voice came:

"Fee, Fi, Fo, Fum,
I smell the blood of an Englishman,
Be he alive or be he dead,
I'll grind his bones to make my bread."

A huge giant came into the room. "Boys, boys, I smell boys," he shouted. "Wife, have I got a boy for breakfast today?"

"No, dear," she said soothingly. "You have got bacon and mushrooms. You must still be smelling the boy you ate last week."

The giant sniffed the air suspiciously but at last sat down. He wolfed his breakfast of bacon and mushrooms, drank a great bucketful of steaming tea, and crunched up a huge slice of toast. Then he got a couple of bags of gold from a cupboard and started counting gold coins. Before long he dropped off to sleep.

Quietly Jack crept out of the oven. Carefully he picked up two gold coins and ran as fast as he could to the top of the beanstalk. He threw the gold down to his mother's garden and climbed after it. At the bottom he found his

mother looking in amazement at the gold coins and the beanstalk. Jack told her of his adventures in the giant's castle, and when she examined the gold she realized he must be speaking the truth.

Jack and his mother used the gold to buy food. But the day came when the money ran out, and Jack decided to climb the beanstalk again.

It was all the same as before, the long climb, the road to the castle, the smell of breakfast, and the giant's wife. But she was not so friendly this time.

"Aren't you the boy who was here before," she asked, "on the day that some gold was stolen from under my husband's nose?"

But Jack convinced her she was wrong and in time her heart softened again and she gave him some breakfast. Once more as Jack was eating, the ground shuddered and the great voice boomed: "'Fee, Fi, Fo, Fum." Quickly, Jack jumped into the oven.

As he entered, the giant bellowed:

> "Fee, Fi, Fo, Fum,
> I smell the blood of an Englishman,
> Be he alive or be he dead,
> I'll grind his bones to make my bread."

The giant's wife put a plate of sizzling sausages before him, telling him he must be mistaken. After breakfast the giant brought a hen from the back room. Every time he said "Lay!" the hen laid an egg of solid gold.

"I must steal that hen, if I can," thought Jack, and he waited until the giant fell asleep. Then he slipped out of the oven, snatched up the hen, and ran for the top of the beanstalk. Keeping the hen under one arm, he scrambled

down as fast as he could until he reached the bottom.

Jack's mother was waiting, but she was not pleased when she saw the hen.

"Another of your silly ideas, is it, bringing an old hen when you might have brought us some gold? I don't know what is to be done with you."

Then Jack set the hen down carefully and commanded "Lay!" just as the giant had done. To his mother's surprise the hen laid an egg of solid gold.

Jack and his mother now lived in great luxury. But in time Jack became a little bored and decided to climb the beanstalk again.

This time he did not risk talking to the giant's wife in case she recognized him. He slipped into the kitchen when she was not looking and hid himself in the log basket. He watched the giant's wife prepare breakfast, and then he heard the giant's roar:

"Fee, Fi, Fo, Fum,
I smell the blood of an Englishman,
Be he alive or be he dead,
I'll grind his bones to make my bread."

"If it's that impudent boy who stole your gold and our magic hen, then I'll help you catch him," said the giant's wife. "Why don't we look in the oven? It's my guess he'll be hiding there."

You may be sure that Jack was glad he was not in the oven. The giant and his wife hunted high and low, but never thought to look in the log basket. At last they gave up, and the giant sat down to breakfast.

After he had eaten, the giant got a harp. When he commanded "Play!" the harp played the most beautiful music. Soon the giant fell asleep, and Jack crept out of the log basket. Quickly he snatched up the harp and ran. But

the harp called out loudly, "Master, save me! Save me!" and the giant woke. With a roar of rage he chased after Jack.

Jack raced down the road toward the beanstalk with the giant's footsteps thundering behind him. When he reached the top of the beanstalk he threw down the harp and started to slither down after it. The giant followed, and now the whole beanstalk shook and shuddered with his weight, and Jack feared for his life. At last he reached the ground, and seizing an ax he chopped at the beanstalk with all his might. *Snap!*

"Look out, mother!" he called as the giant came tumbling down, head first. He lay dead at their feet with the beanstalk on the ground beside them. The harp was broken, but the hen continued to lay golden eggs for Jack and his mother, and they lived happily and in great comfort for a long, long time.

Brer Rabbit's Christmas

Joel Chandler Harris

Once upon a bright clear winter morning Brer Fox stole into Brer Rabbit's garden and dug up a big sackful of his best carrots. Brer Rabbit didn't see him as he was visiting his friend Brer Bear at the time. When he got home he was mighty angry to see his empty carrot-patch.

"Brer Fox! That's who's been here," cried Brer Rabbit, and his whiskers twitched furiously. "Here are his paw marks and some hairs from his tail. All my best winter carrots gone! I'll make him give them back or my name's not Brer Rabbit."

He went along, *lippity lip, clippity clip,* and his little nose wrinkled at the fragrant smell of soup coming from Brer Fox's house.

"Now see here," he called crossly. "I just know it's my carrots you're cooking. I want them back so you'd better open your door."

"Too bad," chuckled Brer Fox. "I'm not opening my door until winter is over. I have plenty of carrots thanks to my kind friend Brer Rabbit, and a stack of other food for Christmas as well. I'm keeping my windows shut and my door bolted, so do go away. I want to enjoy my first bowl of carrot soup in peace."

At this, Brer Rabbit kicked the door, *blim blam!* He hammered on the door, *bangety bang!* It wasn't any use. My, he was in a rage as he turned away. He stomped off, muttering furiously. But soon he grew thoughtful, then he gave a hop or two followed by a little dance. By the time he reached home he was in a mighty good temper. Brer Rabbit had a plan all worked out. He'd get his carrots back and annoy Brer Fox into the bargain!

On Christmas Eve, Brer Rabbit heaved a sack of stones on his shoulder and climbed up onto Brer Fox's roof. He clattered around the chimney making plenty of noise.

"Who's there?" Brer Fox called. "Go away at once. I'm cooking my supper."

"It's Santa Claus," replied Brer Rabbit in a gruff voice. "I've brought a sack full of presents for Brer Fox."

"Oh, that's different," said Brer Fox quickly. "You're most welcome. Come right along down the chimney."

"I can't. I'm stuck," Brer Rabbit said in his gruff Santa Claus voice. Brer Fox unbolted his door and went outside to take a look. Certainly he could see somebody on the roof so he rushed back inside and called,

"Well, Santa Claus, don't trouble to come down the chimney yourself. Just drop the sack of presents and I'll surely catch it."

"Can't. That's stuck too," yelled Brer Rabbit and he smiled to himself. "You'll have to climb up inside your chimney, Brer Fox, then catch hold of the piece of string around the sack and you can haul it down yourself."

"That's easy," Brer Fox cried, "here I come," and he disappeared up the chimney.

Like lightning, Brer Rabbit was off that roof and in through the open doorway. There were his carrots in a sack, and on the table was a fine cooked goose and a huge Christmas pudding. He grabbed them both, stuffed them into the sack and ran. *Chickle, chuckle*, how he did run.

That old Brer Fox struggled up the chimney, higher and higher. He couldn't see any string but he felt it hanging down so he gave a big tug. The sack opened and out tumbled all the stones, *clatter bang, bim bam*, right on Brer Fox's head. My, my, he certainly went down that chimney quickly. Poor Brer Fox! He'd lost his Christmas dinner and the carrots, and now he had a sore head.

That rascally Brer Rabbit laughed and laughed, but he made sure he kept out of Brer Fox's way all that Christmas Day and for some time afterward.

BEAUTY AND THE BEAST

Madame de Beaumont

A rich merchant who had three sons and three daughters lived in a big house in the city. His youngest daughter was so beautiful she was called Beauty by all who knew her. She was as sweet and good as she was beautiful. Sadly, all of the merchant's ships were lost at sea and he and his family had to move to a small cottage in the country. His sons worked hard on the land and Beauty was happy working in the house, but his two elder daughters complained and grumbled all day long, especially about Beauty.

One day news came that a ship had arrived that would make the merchant wealthy again. The merchant set off to the city, and just before he left he said, "Tell me, daughters, what gifts would you like me to bring back for you?"

The two older girls asked for fine clothes and jewels, but Beauty wanted nothing. Realizing this made her sisters look greedy, she thought it best to ask for something. "Bring me a rose, father," she said, "just a beautiful red rose."

When the merchant reached the city he found disaster had struck once more and the ship's cargo was ruined. He took the road home wondering how to break the news to his children. He was so deep in thought that he lost his way. Worse still, it started to snow, and he feared he would never reach home alive. Just as he despaired he noticed lights ahead, and riding toward them he saw a fine castle. The gates stood open and flares were alight in the courtyard. In the stables a stall stood empty with hay in the manger and clean bedding on the floor ready for his horse.

The castle itself seemed to be deserted, but a fire was burning in the dining-hall where a table was laid with food. The merchant ate well, and still finding no one went upstairs to a bedroom which had been prepared. "It is almost as if I were expected," he thought.

In the morning he found clean clothes had been laid out for him and breakfast was on the table in the dining-hall. After he had eaten, he got his horse, and as he rode away he saw a spray of red roses growing from a rose bush. Remembering Beauty's request, and thinking he would be able to bring a present for at least one daughter, he plucked a rose from the bush.

Suddenly a beast-like monster appeared. "Is this how you repay my hospitality?" it roared. "You eat my food, sleep in my guest-room, and then insult me by stealing my flowers. You shall die for this."

The merchant pleaded for his life and begged to see his children once more before he died. At last the beast relented.

"I will spare your life," it said, "if one of your daughters will come here willingly and die for you. Otherwise you must promise to return within three months and die yourself."

The merchant agreed to return and went on his way. At home his children listened with sorrow to his tales of the lost cargo and his promise to the monster. His two elder daughters turned on Beauty, saying, "Your stupid request for a rose has brought all this trouble on us. It is your fault that father must die."

When the three months were up Beauty insisted on going to the castle with her father, pretending only to ride with him for company on the journey. The beast met them and asked Beauty if she had come of her own accord, and she told him she had.

"Good," he said. "Now your father can go home and you will stay with me."

"What shall I call you?" she asked bravely.

"You may call me Beast," he replied.

Certainly he was very ugly and it seemed a good name for him. Beauty waved a sad farewell to her father. But she was happy that at least she had saved his life.

As Beauty wandered through the castle she found many lovely rooms and beautiful courtyards with gardens. At last she came to a room which was surely meant just for her. It had many of her favorite books and objects in it. On the wall hung a beautiful mirror and to her surprise, as she looked into it, she saw her father arriving back at their home and her brothers and sisters greeting him. The picture only lasted a few seconds then faded. "This Beast may be ugly, but he is certainly kind," she thought. "He gives me all the things I like and allows me to know how my family is without me."

That night at supper the Beast joined her at the candle-lit table. He sat and stared at her. At the end of

the meal he asked: "Will you marry me?"

Beauty was startled by the question but said as gently as she could, "No, Beast, you are kind but I cannot marry you."

Each day it was the same. Beauty had everything she wanted during the day and each evening the Beast asked her to marry him, and she always said no.

One night Beauty dreamed that her father lay sick. She asked the Beast if she could go to him, and he refused, saying that if she left him he would die of loneliness. But when he saw how unhappy Beauty was, he said:

"If you go to your family, will you return within a week?"

"Of course," Beauty replied.

"Very well, just place this ring on your dressing table the night you wish to return, and you shall come back

here. But do not stay away longer than a week, or I shall die.''

The next morning Beauty awoke to find herself in her own home. Her father was indeed sick, but Beauty nursed him lovingly. Beauty's sisters were jealous once more. They thought that if she stayed at home longer than a week the Beast would kill her. So they pretended to love her and told her how much they had missed her. Before Beauty knew what had happened ten days had passed. Then she had a dream that the Beast was lying still as though he were dead by the lake near his castle.

"I must return at once," she cried and she placed her ring on the dressing table.

The next morning she found herself once more in the Beast's castle. All that day she expected to see him, but he never came. "I have killed the Beast," she cried, "I have killed him." Then she remembered that in her dream he had been by the lake and quickly she ran there. He lay still as death, down by the water's edge.

"Oh, Beast!" she wept, "Oh, Beast! I did not mean to stay away so long. Please do not die. Please come back to me. You are so good and kind." She knelt and kissed his ugly head.

Suddenly no Beast was there, but a handsome prince stood before her. "Beauty, my dear one," he said. "I was bewitched by a spell that could only be broken when a beautiful girl loved me and wanted me in spite of my ugliness. When you kissed me just now you broke the enchantment."

Beauty rode with the prince to her father's house, and then they all went together to the prince's kingdom. There he and Beauty were married. In time they became king and queen, and ruled for many happy years.

THE LITTLE RED HEN

English Traditional

Once upon a time there was a little red hen. She lived with a pig, a duck, and a cat.

They all lived in a pretty little house, which the little red hen liked to keep clean and neat. The little red hen worked hard at her jobs all day. The others never helped. Although they said they meant to, they were all far too lazy. The pig liked to grunt in the mud outside, the duck used to swim in the pond all day, and the cat enjoyed lying in the sun, purring.

One day, the little red hen was working in the garden when she found a grain of wheat.

"Who will plant this grain of wheat?" she asked.

"Not I," grunted the pig from his muddy patch in the garden.

"Not I," quacked the duck from her pond.

"Not I," purred the cat from his place in the sun.

So the little red hen went to look for a nice piece of ground, scratched it with her feet, and planted the grain of wheat.

During the summer the grain of wheat grew. First it grew into a tall green stalk, then it ripened in the sun until it had turned a beautiful golden color. The little red hen saw that the wheat was ready for cutting.

"Who will help me cut the wheat?" asked the little red hen.

"Not I," grunted the pig from his muddy patch in the garden.

"Not I," quacked the duck from her pond.

"Not I," purred the cat from his place in the sun.

"Very well then, I will cut it myself," said the little red hen. Carefully she cut the stalk and took out all the grains of wheat from the husks.

"Who will take the wheat to the mill, so that it can be ground into flour?" asked the little red hen.

"Not I," grunted the pig from his muddy patch in the garden.

"Not I," quacked the duck from her pond.

"Not I," purred the cat from his place in the sun.

So the little red hen took the wheat to the mill herself, and asked the miller if he would be so kind as to grind it into flour.

In time the miller sent a little bag of flour down to the house where the little red hen lived with the pig and the duck and the cat.

"Who will help me to make the flour into bread?" asked the little red hen.

"Not I," grunted the pig from his muddy patch in the garden.

"Not I," quacked the duck from her pond.

"Not I," purred the cat from his place in the sun.

"Very well," said the little red hen. "I shall make the bread myself." She went into her neat little kitchen. She mixed the flour into dough. She kneaded the dough and put it into the oven to bake.

Soon there was a wonderful smell of hot fresh bread. It filled all the corners of the house and wafted out into the garden. The pig came into the kitchen from his muddy patch in the garden, the duck came in from the pond, and the cat left his place in the sun. When the little red hen opened the oven door the dough had risen up and had turned into the nicest, most delicious looking loaf of bread any of them had seen.

"Who is going to eat this bread?" asked the little red hen.

"I will," grunted the pig.

"I will," quacked the duck.

"I will," purred the cat.

"Oh no, you won't," said the little red hen. "I planted the seed, I cut the wheat, I took it to the mill to be made into flour, and I made the bread, all by myself. I shall now eat the loaf all by myself."

The pig, the duck, and the cat all stood and watched as the little red hen ate the loaf all by herself. It was delicious and she enjoyed it, right to the very last crumb.

THE LITTLE MERMAID

Hans Andersen

Deep under the sea, colorful fish glide among strange plants, which wave gently to and fro in the crystal-clear water. In the deepest part, which no human has ever visited, the mer-people live. The mer-king's palace has coral walls and a roof of oyster shells that open and close gently with the waves, each one hiding a gleaming pearl. Now the mer-king had six beautiful daughters, but the youngest mermaid was the loveliest of all. Her eyes were deepest sea-blue, her skin like a rose petal, and the scales on her mermaid tail shone like precious jewels.

The mermaid loved hearing about the world above the sea which her grandmother described to her.

"When you are fifteen," her grandmother said, "you may swim to the top of the ocean and see these wonderful things for yourself."

How impatiently she waited for her fifteenth birthday. At last the day arrived. She combed her long golden hair, she polished the scales on her tail, then waving to her sisters she put her arms together and glided, up, up through the waves.

When she lifted her head above the water, she saw a big sailing ship with a large anchor and chain holding it firmly in place. She noticed sailors lighting pretty lanterns along the deck. The mermaid swam swiftly to a porthole in the captain's cabin, and when the waves lifted her up, she peeped inside. There were many fine gentlemen, but the finest of all was a prince. He was laughing and shaking hands with everyone while soft music played. She had never seen anyone like him before. She could not keep her eyes away from him.

Suddenly the sky darkened and the ship started to roll. The waves grew mountainous, thunder rolled around, and the ship was tossed up and then plunged down into the stormy seas. Then the ship's mast snapped and the ship rolled right over and started to sink. At first the mermaid felt happy, for now the prince would sink to her father's palace.

"But humans can't live under the sea," she remembered. "I must save his life somehow." And she swam through the wreckage until she spied the prince, just as he was slipping beneath the waves. His eyes were closed because he had no strength left. He was drowning.

Quickly, the mermaid seized his head and held it above water. Then she rested on a huge wave and let it carry her and the prince safely away from the wrecked ship.

When morning came the storm died away and the warm sun appeared. The mermaid still held the prince but he did not move. She touched his face gently and kissed his cold lips. His eyes did not open. "Wake up, please don't die," she whispered.

Now she could see dry land ahead and, still clutching the prince, she swam into a pretty bay with calm clear water. Tenderly she laid the prince on the warm golden sand away from the waves. At that moment she saw some girls walking along the sands. Quickly she swam away. She covered herself with seaweed and hid behind some rocks and watched the prince anxiously. "Please wake up," she begged.

Soon one girl noticed him and called for help. He opened his eyes and smiled at the girl who had found him. As the prince was carried away the mermaid sadly dived into the waves and swam back to the mer-king's palace.

"What did you see?" her sisters asked. She told them nothing, but all day long she dreamed quietly by herself.

At night she often swam to Prince Bay as she called it, but she never saw the prince there. She became sadder each time she swam back home.

The mermaid now had only one wish — to be a human. She started to ask her grandmother many questions: "Do humans live for ever? Do they die like us?"

"They die," came the reply, "only human lives are shorter than ours. We live for three hundred years, and then we turn into foam upon the waves. Humans have souls that live forever in the skies."

"Why can't I be like that?" sighed the mermaid. "I'd like to exchange my three hundred years for one day of human life. I'd rather live in the sky forever than change into foam!"

"That's no way to speak," said her grandmother.

"Can't I ever get this human immortal soul?" the mermaid asked over and over again until in the end her grandmother said: "There is only one way. If a man loved you more than anyone or anything else, then his soul could run into you and you would be immortal. But this won't happen because humans say that our tails are ugly. They only like something they call 'legs'."

She glided away and the little mermaid looked sadly at her lovely tail. She couldn't forget the prince. Somehow she must become human. "I'll ask the sea-witch to help," she exclaimed. Off she swam to the whirlpool where the evil witch lived. The waters bubbled and hissed, but she dived bravely through. There was dirty gray sand everywhere and a hut made from the bones of ship-wrecked sailors. Gray slugs crawled around, and in the middle sat a fearsome creature.

"So, mermaid," she cackled, "first, you want to lose your beautiful tail. Then you want the prince to love you

and give you an immortal soul." She laughed so horribly that even the slugs scuttled away. "I'll mix something for you to drink when you've reached the shore. Your tail will shrink and divide into two funny things called legs. You will have a terrible pain like a knife cutting through you, and this pain will never leave you. You will always be beautiful and you'll be the best dancer in the world, but every step you take will be painful."

"I'll bear anything for the prince," the mermaid said bravely.

"There's something else," warned the witch. "Once you've become a human you can never be a mermaid again. You can't return to your father's palace. If the prince doesn't love you, you cannot be immortal. You will

36

turn into foam the day after he marries someone else."

The mermaid trembled. "I'll do it," she whispered.

"I haven't finished," the witch said. "In return for this drink I demand that you give me your voice, for it is the sweetest of all. That shall be my payment."

"But how will I speak and charm the prince?"

"You're beautiful, you'll dance, you'll smile. Come, put out your tongue."

The little mermaid shivered but her mind was made up. From then on she could neither speak nor sing.

The witch scratched a few drops of blood from her scrawny arms, added snails and worms, and poured everything into a pot. Groans, strange shapes, and a horrible smell rose from the pot. Then, when the liquid inside was clear, the witch handed it to her. She took it carefully and swam through the whirlpool.

She found the shore nearest to the prince's palace, and as the sun was rising she drank the magic liquid. A pain worse than a thousand sharp cuts went through her, and she fainted on the sand. She woke with a jump and the terrible pain came back. She groaned inside herself. Then she saw the prince of her dreams gazing down at her, greatly astonished. She looked away and at once she saw that her shimmering tail had gone. Her golden hair was now covering two long and graceful legs.

"Who are you? Where did you come from?" asked the prince, but she could only smile in reply. He took her by the hand toward his palace — but exactly as the witch had said, every step was like touching red-hot metal. She could not cry out, yet she walked so gracefully that everyone gazed at her as she passed by.

The prince ordered his servants to bring rich satin and silk dresses for her. Even though she could not speak, everyone thought her the loveliest girl in the palace. She heard many girls singing sweet songs to the prince, who thanked them kindly. She felt sad because she used to sing far far better than any of these girls. Some other girls started to dance. The little mermaid shook out her long hair and moved across the floor. Her steps were perfect and her hands and arms moved gracefully to the music. The prince clapped and she danced on and on though terrible pains shot through her feet.

The prince gave her a wonderful room filled with rich furniture and every day they went riding together.

The prince loved the mermaid, but he did not think of marrying her. "You are the sweetest girl I know," he often said. "You remind me of a maiden who saved my life when my ship was wrecked. I only saw her once, yet I

cannot forget her. She is the only one I can truly love."

"He little knows that I carried him through the waves to the shore, that I saved his life," she sighed to herself.

One day the king ordered the prince to visit the kingdom of an old friend who had one daughter.

"I must obey my father," he told the little mermaid, "but nobody can make me marry this princess. You are more like my lost love, so if I must get married, I'll marry you." He kissed her gently.

They sailed away with many courtiers to the distant land. When they had landed they were led toward the royal palace. The princess came out to meet them.

"It is my true love," exclaimed the prince. "You're the one who saved my life, let us be married at once!" He kissed her hand.

"How happy I am," he said to the mermaid. "I know you will share my joy for I know that you love me truly."

The little mermaid's heart broke then. The very next day church bells rang, trumpets sounded, and fireworks went off as the prince and princess were married.

That night everyone went on board the prince's ship, and soon there was dancing and soft music. The little mermaid danced more beautifully than ever. She forgot her fearful pain because she knew this was the last night she would see the prince.

At midnight, the music stopped and the prince led his bride away. All was silent, yet the little mermaid stayed awake, waiting for the dawn. Suddenly she saw her sisters, but where was their long golden hair?

"We gave our hair to the witch," they whispered, "to make her help you. This is what she says you must do. Take this dagger, and before the sun rises plunge it deep into the prince's heart. Then your fishtail will return and you will turn into a mermaid again. Remember, it is your life or his. Hurry! Kill him quickly. Do not see the sun or it will be too late." With this they sank beneath the waves.

The little mermaid crept inside the purple tent where the happy couple were sleeping peacefully. As she kissed the prince she held the dagger over his heart — then she hurled it far away into the sea. She looked once more at the prince. Then she dived into the sea, where her body turned into white sparkling foam. She heard sweet music. She saw a thousand delicate shapes floating and singing around her. She felt that she was floating.

"Where am I going? Who are you?" she asked.

"We are daughters of the air," they sang. "Mermaids are given souls if a human loves them, but we can only have one if we do good deeds for three hundred years. We'll help you to get your soul."

She saw the prince searching for her. He gazed sadly over the sea as if he knew what had happened. Unseen, she kissed him, and smiling sweetly, she rose into the golden clouds with the daughters of the air. She whispered joyfully: "In three hundred years, I shall join my prince again in Heaven."

HENNY PENNY

English Traditional

One day Henny Penny was scratching in the farmyard looking for something good to eat when, suddenly, something hit her on the head.

"My goodness me!" she said. "The sky must be falling down. I must go and tell the king."

She had not gone far when she met her friend Cocky Locky.

"Where are you going in such a hurry?" he called out.

"I am going to tell the king that the sky is falling down," said Henny Penny.

"I will come with you," said Cocky Locky.

So Henny Penny and Cocky Locky hurried along together toward the king's palace. On the way they saw Ducky Lucky swimming on the pond. "Where are you going?" he called out.

"We are going to tell the king the sky is falling down," replied Henny Penny. "We must go quickly, as there is no time to lose."

"I will come with you," said Ducky Lucky, shaking the water off his feathers.

So Henny Penny, Cocky Locky, and Ducky Lucky hurried on together toward the king's palace. On the way they met Goosey Loosey, who called out, "Where are you all going in such a hurry?"

"We are on our way to tell the king the sky is falling down," said Henny Penny.

"I will come with you," said Goosey Loosey.

So Henny Penny, Cocky Locky, Ducky Lucky, and

Goosey Loosey hurried on together toward the king's palace.

Around the next corner they met Turkey Lurkey. "Where are you all going on this fine day?" she called out to them.

"It won't be a fine day for long," replied Henny Penny. "The sky is falling down, and we are hurrying to tell the king."

"I will come with you," said Turkey Lurkey.

So Henny Penny, Cocky Locky, Ducky Lucky, Goosey Loosey, and Turkey Lurkey all went on toward the king's palace.

Now on their way they met Foxy Loxy who asked, "Where are you going in such a hurry?"

"We are going to the king's palace to tell him the sky is falling down," replied Henny Penny.

"That is a very important message," said Foxy Loxy.

"I will come with you. In fact if you follow me I can show you a short cut to the king's palace, so you will get there sooner."

So Henny Penny, Cocky Locky, Ducky Lucky, Goosey Loosey, and Turkey Lurkey all followed Foxy Loxy. He led them to the wood, and up to a dark hole, which was the door to his home. Inside his wife and five hungry children were waiting for him to bring home some dinner.

That, I am sorry to say, was the end of Cocky Locky, Ducky Lucky, Goosey Loosey, and Turkey Lurkey, for one by one they all followed Foxy Loxy into his home, and they were all eaten up by the hungry fox family.

Henny Penny was the last to enter the Fox's hole and she heard Cocky Locky crowing in alarm in front of her. Squawking with fright and scattering feathers, she turned and ran as fast as she could for the safety of her own farmyard. There she stayed and she never did tell the king that the sky was falling down.

THE THREE LITTLE PIGS

English Traditional

Once upon a time there were three little pigs. One day they set out from the farm where they had been born. They were going out into the world to start new lives and enjoy any adventures that might come their way.

The first little pig met a man carrying some straw, and he asked him if he might have some to build himself a house.

"Of course, little pig," said the man. He gave the little pig a big bundle of straw, and the little pig built himself a beautiful house of golden straw.

A big bad wolf lived nearby. He came along and saw the new house and, feeling very hungry and thinking he would like to eat a little pig for supper, he called out,

"Little pig, little pig, let me come in." To which the little pig replied,

"No, no, by the hair of my chinny chin chin,
I'll not let you in!"
So the wolf shouted very crossly,

"Then I'll huff and I'll puff,
Till I blow your house in!"
And he huffed and he puffed, and he HUFFED and he PUFFED until the house of straw fell in, and the wolf ate the little pig for his supper that evening.

The second little pig was walking along the road when he met a man with a load of wood. "Please Sir," he said, "can you let me have some of that wood so that I can build a house?"

"Of course," said the man, and he gave him a big pile of wood. In no time at all, the little pig had built himself a nice house. The next evening, along came the same wolf. When he saw another little pig, this time in a wooden house, he called out.

"Little pig, little pig, let me come in."
To which the pig replied,
"No, no, by the hair of my chinny chin chin,
I'll not let you in!"
So the wolf shouted,
"Then I'll huff and I'll puff,
Till I blow your house in!"
And he huffed and he puffed and he HUFFED and he PUFFED until the house fell in and the wolf gobbled up the little pig for his supper.

The third little pig met a man with a cartload of bricks. "Please Sir, can I have some bricks to build myself a house?" he asked, and when the man had given him some, he built himself a sturdy house with bricks.

The big bad wolf came along, and he licked his lips as he thought about the third little pig. He called out,

"Little pig, little pig, let me come in!"

And the little pig called back,

"No, no, by the hair of my chinny chin chin,
I'll not let you in!"

So the wolf shouted,

"Then I'll huff and I'll puff,
Till I blow your house in!"

And the wolf huffed and he puffed, and he HUFFED and he PUFFED, and he HUFFED again and PUFFED again, but still the house, which had been so well built with bricks, did not blow in, no matter how hard the wolf tried.

The wolf went away to think about how he could trick the little pig, and he came back and called through the window of the brick house, "Little pig, there are some marvelous turnips in the farmer's field. Shall we go there tomorrow morning at six o'clock and get some?"

The little pig thought this was a good idea, since he was very fond of turnips, but he went at five o'clock, not six o'clock, and collected all the turnips he needed before the wolf arrived.

The wolf was furious, but he thought he would try another trick. He told the little pig about the apples in the farmer's orchard and suggested they both go to get some at five o'clock the next morning. The little pig agreed, and went as before, an hour earlier. But this time the wolf came early too and arrived while the little pig was still in the apple tree. The little pig pretended to be pleased to see him and threw an apple down to the wolf. While the wolf was picking it up, the little pig jumped down the tree and got into a barrel. He rolled quickly down the hill inside this barrel to his house of bricks and rushed in and bolted the door.

The wolf was very angry that the little pig had gotten the better of him again and chased him in the barrel back to his house. When he got there he climbed onto the roof, intending to come down the chimney and catch the little pig that way. The little pig was waiting for him, however, with a large cauldron of boiling water on the fire. The wolf came down the chimney and fell into the cauldron with a big SPLASH, and the little pig quickly put the lid on it.

The wicked wolf was never seen again, and the little pig lived happily in his brick house for many many years.

ALADDIN AND THE WONDERFUL LAMP

Arabian Nights

Far off in a beautiful city in China a ragged urchin called Aladdin used to play in the street. His father, a poor tailor, tried to make him work, but Aladdin was lazy and disobedient, and refused even to help in his father's shop. Even after his father died Aladdin still preferred to roam in the streets with his friends, and did not feel ashamed to eat the food his mother bought with the money she earned by spinning cotton.

One day a wealthy stranger came to the city. He noticed Aladdin in the street and thought, "That lad looks as though he has no purpose in life. It will not matter if I use him, then kill him."

The stranger quickly found out that Aladdin's father was dead. He called Aladdin over to him.

"Greetings, nephew," he said, "I am your father's brother. I have returned to China only to find my dear brother, Mustapha, is dead. Take this money and tell your mother I shall visit her."

Aladdin's mother was puzzled when Aladdin told her the stranger's message. "You have no uncle," she said. "I don't understand why this man should give us money."

The next day the stranger came to their house and talked about how he had loved his brother and offered to buy a fine shop where Aladdin could sell beautiful things to the rich people in the city. He gave Aladdin some new clothes and in a short while Aladdin's mother began to believe this man was a relation.

The stranger now invited Aladdin to go with him to

the rich part of the city. Together they walked through beautiful gardens and parks where Aladdin had never been before. At last the stranger showed Aladdin a flat stone with an iron ring set into it.

"Lift this stone for me, nephew," he said, "and go into the cavern below. Walk through three caves where you will see gold and silver stored. Do not touch it. You will then pass through a garden full of wonderful fruit and beyond the trees you will find a lamp. Pour out the oil and bring the lamp to me. Pick some of the fruit on your return if you wish."

Aladdin lifted the stone and saw some steps leading down into a cave. He was frightened to go down but the stranger placed a gold ring with a great green emerald on his finger.

"Take this ring as a gift," he said, "but you must go or I shall not buy you a shop."

Now the stranger was in fact a magician. He had read about a lamp with magical powers, and he had traveled far to find it. He knew the magic would not work for him unless the lamp was fetched from the cavern and handed to him by someone else. After Aladdin had brought him the lamp the magician planned to shut him in the cave to die.

Down in the cavern Aladdin found all as he had been told. He hurried through the rooms filled with silver and gold, and passed through the garden where the trees were hung with shimmering fruit of all colors. At the far end stood an old lamp. Aladdin took it, poured out the oil, and then picked some of the dazzling fruit from the trees as the magician had suggested. To his surprise they were all made from stones. Aladdin took as many as he could carry and returned to the steps.

"Give me the lamp," demanded the magician as soon as Aladdin came into sight.

"Help me out first," replied Aladdin who could not hand him the lamp because his arms were so full. They argued fiercely until *crash*, the stone slab fell back into place. The magician could not move the stone from the outside, nor Aladdin from within. He was trapped. The magician knew he had failed in his quest and decided to leave the country at once.

For two days Aladdin tried to get out of the cave. He became weak with hunger and thirst and finally as he sat in despair he rubbed his hands together. By chance he rubbed the gold ring that the stranger had given him. There was a blinding flash and a genie appeared. "I am the genie of the ring. What can I do for you, master?"

"Get me out of here," Aladdin gasped. He was terrified of the great burning spirit of the genie glowing in the cavern. Before he knew what had happened he was standing on the ground above the entrance to the cavern. Of the stone slab there was no sign. Aladdin set off for home and collapsed with hunger as he entered the house.

His mother was overjoyed to see him. She gave him all the scraps of food she had and when she said she had no more Aladdin suggested selling the lamp to buy some food.

"I'll get a better price for it, if it's clean," she thought, and she rubbed the lamp with a cloth. In a flash the genie appeared. Aladdin's mother fainted in horror but Aladdin seized the lamp. When the genie saw him with the lamp it said:

"I am the genie of the lamp. What can I do for you, master?"

"Get me some food," ordered Aladdin.

By the time his mother had recovered there were twelve silver dishes of food and twelve silver cups on the table. Aladdin and his mother ate as they had never eaten before. They had enough for several days, and then Aladdin began to sell the silver dishes and cups. He and his mother lived comfortably in this way for some time.

Then it happened that Aladdin saw the sultan's daughter, Princess Badroulboudoir. Aladdin loved her at first sight and sent his mother to the sultan's court to ask the sultan permission for the princess to marry him. He told her to take as a gift the stone fruits he had brought from the cave.

It was several days before Aladdin's mother could speak with the sultan, but at last she was able to give him the stone fruits. The sultan was truly amazed.

"Your son has such fine jewels he would make a good husband for my daughter, I am sure," he told Aladdin's mother.

But the sultan's chief courtier was jealous. He wanted his son to marry the princess. Quickly, he advised the

sultan to say he would decide on the marriage in three months' time. Aladdin was happy when he heard the news.

But at the palace, the chief courtier spoke against Aladdin and when Aladdin's mother returned in three months, the sultan asked her: "Can your son send me forty golden bowls full of jewels like the ones he sent before only this time carried by forty servants?"

Aladdin rubbed the lamp once more and before long forty servants each carrying a gold bowl filled with sparkling jewels were assembled in the courtyard of their little house.

When the sultan saw them, he said:

"I am sure now that the owner of these riches will make a fine husband for my daughter."

But the chief courtier suggested yet another test. "Ask the woman," he said, "if her son has a palace fit for your daughter to live in."

"I'll give him the land and he can build a new palace," declared the sultan, and he presented Aladdin with land in front of his own palace.

Aladdin summoned the genie of the lamp once more. Overnight the most amazing palace appeared with walls of gold and silver, huge windows, beautiful halls, and courtyards and rooms filled with treasures. A carpet of red velvet was laid from the old palace to the new, for the princess to walk on to her new home. Aladdin then asked the genie for some fine clothes for himself and his mother, and a glorious wedding took place.

Aladdin took care always to keep the wonderful lamp safe. One day the princess gave it to an old beggar who was the magician in disguise, but that story will have to keep for another time.

SNOW WHITE AND THE SEVEN DWARFS

Grimm Brothers

One winter's day, when the snow was falling, a beautiful queen sat sewing by a window. As she looked out onto the white garden she saw a black raven, and while she looked at it she accidentally pricked her finger with the needle. When she saw the drop of blood she thought to herself, "How wonderful it would be if I could have a little girl whose skin was as white as the snow out there, her hair as black as the raven, and her lips as red as this drop of blood."

Not long afterward the queen had a baby daughter, and when she saw her jet black hair, snowy white skin, and red red lips she remembered her wish and called her Snow White.

Snow White grew up to be a pretty child, but sadly, after a few years, her mother died and her father married again. The new queen, Snow White's step-mother, was a beautiful woman too, but she was very vain. More than anything else she wanted to be certain that she was the most beautiful woman in the world. She had a magic mirror, and she used to look at herself in it each day and say:

>*"Mirror, mirror on the wall,*
>*Who is the fairest one of all?"*

and the mirror would always reply,

>*"You, oh Queen, are the fairest one of all."*

The queen would smile when she heard this for she knew the mirror never failed to speak the truth.

The years passed. Each year Snow White grew

prettier and prettier, until one day, her stepmother looked in the magic mirror and said,

> *"Mirror, mirror on the wall,*
> *Who is the fairest one of all?"*

and the mirror replied,

> *"You, oh Queen, are fair, 'tis true,*
> *But Snow White is fairer now than you."*

The queen was angry and jealous. In a terrible rage she decided that Snow White should be killed.

She called for a hunter and told him to take Snow White far into the forest and to kill her there. In order to prove that Snow White was indeed dead, she commanded him to cut out Snow White's heart and bring it back to her. The hunter was very sad. Like everyone in the king's household he loved Snow White, but he knew he must obey his orders. He took her deep into the forest and, as he drew his knife, Snow White fell to her knees.

"Please spare my life," she begged. "Leave me here. I'll never return to the palace, I promise." The hunter agreed gladly. He was sure the queen would never know he had disobeyed her. He killed a young deer and cut out its heart and took this to the queen, pretending it was Snow White's heart.

Poor Snow White was tired, lonely, and hungry in the forest. She wandered through the trees, hoping she would find enough berries and nuts to keep herself alive. Then she came to a clearing and found a little house. She thought it must be a woodman's cottage where she might be able to stay, so she knocked at the door. When there was no answer, she opened it and went inside.

There she saw a room all spick and span with a long table laid with seven places — seven knives and forks, seven wooden plates and drinking cups, and on the plates and in the cups were food and drink. Snow White was so hungry she could not bear to leave the food untouched so she took a little from each plate and each cup. She did not want to empty one person's plate and cup only.

Beyond the table were seven little beds all neatly made. She tried out some of them, and when she found one that was comfortable, she fell into a deep sleep, for she was exhausted by her long journey through the forest.

The cottage was the home of seven dwarfs. All day long they worked in a nearby mine digging diamonds from deep inside the mountain. When they returned home that evening, they were amazed to see that someone had been into their cottage and had taken some food and drink from each place at their table. They were also surprised to find their beds disturbed, until one dwarf called out that he had found a lovely girl asleep on his bed. The Seven Dwarfs gathered around her, holding their candles high, as they marveled at her beauty. But they decided to leave her sleeping for they were kind men.

The next morning Snow White awoke and met the dwarfs, and she told them her story. When she explained how she now had no home, the dwarfs immediately asked her whether she would like to stay with them.

"With all my heart, I'd love to do that," Snow White replied, happy that she now had a home, and she hoped she could be of help to these kind little people.

The dwarfs suspected that Snow White's stepmother, the wicked queen, had magic powers and they were worried that she would find out that Snow White had not been killed by the hunter. They warned Snow White that when she was alone all day she should be wary of strangers who might come to the cottage.

Back at the palace the queen welcomed the hunter when he returned with the deer's heart. She was happy that now she was once more the most beautiful woman in the world. As soon as she was alone, she looked in her magic mirror and said, confidently,

"Mirror, mirror on the wall,
Who is the fairest one of all?"

57

To her horror, the mirror replied,
> *"You, oh Queen, are fair, 'tis true,*
> *But Snow White is fairer still than you."*

The queen trembled with anger as she realized that the hunter had tricked her. She decided that she would now find Snow White and kill her herself.

The queen disguised herself as an old pedlar woman with a tray of ribbons and pretty things to sell and she set out into the forest. When she came to the dwarfs' cottage in the clearing, she knocked and smiled a wicked smile when she saw Snow White come to the door.

"Why, pretty maid," she said pleasantly, "won't you buy some of the wares I have to sell? Would you like some ribbons or buttons, some buckles, a new lacing for your dress perhaps?"

Snow White looked eagerly at the tray.

The queen could see that she was tempted by the pretty lacing and so she asked if she could help to tie it on for her. Then she pulled the lacing so tight that Snow White could not breathe, and fell to the floor, as if she were dead. The queen hurried back to her palace, sure that this time Snow White was really dead.

When the dwarfs came home that evening, they found Snow White lying on the floor, deathly pale and still. Horrified, they gathered around her. Then one of them spotted that she had a new lacing on her dress, and that it was tied very tightly. Quickly they cut it. Immediately Snow White began to breathe again and color came back to her cheeks. All seven dwarfs heaved a tremendous sigh of relief as by now they loved her dearly. After this they begged Snow White to allow no strangers into the cottage while she was alone, and Snow White promised she would do as they said.

Once again in the palace the queen asked the mirror,

> *"Mirror, mirror on the wall,*
> *Who is the fairest one of all?"*

And the mirror replied,

> *"You, oh Queen, are fair, 'tis true,*
> *But Snow White is fairer still than you."*

The queen was speechless with rage. She realized that once more her plans to kill Snow White had failed. She made up her mind to try again.

She chose an apple with one rosy-red side and one yellow side. Carefully she inserted poison into the red part of the apple. Then, disguised as a peasant woman, she set out once more into the forest.

When she knocked at the cottage door, the queen was quick to explain she had not come to sell anything. She guessed that Snow White would have been warned not to buy from anybody who came by. She simply chatted to Snow White and as Snow White became more at ease she offered her an apple as a present. Snow White was tempted, but she refused, saying she had been told not to accept anything from strangers.

"Let me show you how harmless it is," said the disguised queen. "I will take a bite, and if I come to no harm, you will see it is safe for you too."

She knew the yellow side was not poisoned and took a bite from there. Thinking it harmless, Snow White stretched out her hand for the apple and also took a bite, but from the rosy-red side.

At once Snow White was affected by the poison and fell down as though dead. That evening when the dwarfs returned they were quite unable to revive her. They turned her over to see if her dress had been laced too tightly. But they could find nothing different about her. They watched over her through the night, but when morning came she still lay without any sign of life, and they decided she must be dead. Weeping bitterly, they laid her in a coffin and placed a glass lid over the top so that all could admire her beauty, even though she was dead. Then they carried the coffin to the top of a hill where they took turns to stand guard.

The queen was delighted that day when she looked in her mirror and asked,

> *"Mirror, mirror on the wall,*
> *Who is the fairest one of all?"*

and the mirror replied,

> *"You, oh Queen, are the fairest one of all."*

How cruelly she laughed when she heard those words.

Not long after this a prince came riding through the forest and came to the hill where Snow White lay in her glass-topped coffin. She looked so beautiful that he loved her at once and he asked the dwarfs if he might have the coffin and take it to his castle. The dwarfs would not allow him to do this, but they did let the prince kiss her.

As the prince kissed Snow White gently, he moved her head. The piece of poisoned apple fell from her lips. She stirred and then she stretched a little. Slowly she came back to life. Snow White saw the handsome prince kneeling on the ground beside her and fell in love with him immediately.

Then the queen far away in the palace heard from the mirror,

> *"You, oh Queen, are fair, tis true,*
> *But Snow White is fairer still than you."*

She was furious that Snow White had escaped death once more. And now the king discovered what mischief she had been up to, and he banished her from his land. No one ever saw her or her mirror again.

As for Snow White, she said farewell to her kind friends the dwarfs and rode away on the back of the prince's horse. At his castle they were married, and they both lived happily forever afterward.

THE GREAT BIG TURNIP

Russian Traditional

Once upon a time, in Russia, an old man planted some turnip seeds. Each year he grew good turnips, but this year he was especially proud of one very big turnip. He left it in the ground longer than the others and watched with amazement and delight as it grew bigger and bigger. It grew so big that no one could remember ever having seen such a huge turnip before.

At last it stopped growing, and the old man decided that the time had come to pull it up. He took hold of the leaves of the great big turnip and pulled and pulled, but the turnip did not move.

So the old man called his wife to come and help him. The old woman pulled the old man, and the old man pulled the turnip. Together they pulled and pulled, but the turnip did not move.

So the old woman called her granddaughter to come and help. The granddaughter pulled the old woman, the old woman pulled the old man, and the old man pulled the turnip. Still the turnip did not move.

The granddaughter called to the dog to come and help. The dog pulled the granddaughter, the granddaughter pulled the old woman, the old woman pulled the old man, and the old man pulled the turnip. But the great big turnip stayed firmly in the ground.

The dog called to the cat to come and help pull up the turnip. The cat pulled the dog, the dog pulled the granddaughter, the granddaughter pulled the old woman, the old woman pulled the old man, and the old man pulled the turnip. They all pulled and pulled as hard as they could, but still the turnip did not move.

Then the cat called to a mouse to come and help pull up the great big turnip. The mouse pulled the cat, the cat pulled the dog, the dog pulled the granddaughter, the granddaughter pulled the old woman, the old woman pulled the old man, and he pulled the big turnip. Together they pulled and pulled and pulled as hard as they could.

Suddenly, the great big turnip came out of the ground, and everyone fell over.

SLEEPING BEAUTY

Charles Perrault

There once lived a king and queen who had no children, which made them very sad. Then one day, to the queen's delight, she found she was going to have a baby. She and the king looked forward with great excitement to the day of the baby's birth.

When the time came, a lovely daughter was born, and they arranged a large party for her Christening. As well as lots of other guests, they invited twelve fairies, knowing they would make wishes for their little daughter, the princess.

At the Christening party, the guests and the fairies all agreed that the princess was a beautiful baby. One fairy wished on her the gift of Happiness, another Beauty, others Health, Contentment, Wisdom, Goodness . . . Eleven fairies had made their wishes when suddenly the doors of the castle flew open and in swept a thirteenth fairy. She was furious that she had not been invited to the Christening party, and as she looked around a shiver ran down everyone's spine. They could feel she was evil. She waved her wand over the baby's cradle and cast a spell, not a wish.

"On her sixteenth birthday," she hissed, "the princess will prick herself with a spindle. And she will die." With that a terrible hush fell over the crowd.

The twelfth fairy still had to make her wish and she hesitated. She had been going to wish the gift of Joy for the baby, but now she wanted to stop the princess from dying on her sixteenth birthday. Her magic was not

64

strong enough to break the wicked spell, but she tried to weaken the evil. She wished that the princess would fall asleep for a hundred years instead of dying.

Over the years the princess grew into the happiest, kindest, and most beautiful child anyone had ever seen. It seemed as though all the wishes of the first eleven fairies had come true. The king and queen decided they could prevent the wicked fairy's spell from working by making sure that the princess never saw a spindle.

So they banned all spinning from the land. All the flax and wool in their country had to be sent elsewhere to be spun. On their daughter's sixteenth birthday they held a party for the princess in their castle. They felt sure this would protect her from the danger of finding a spindle on her sixteenth birthday.

People came from far and wide to the grand birthday ball for the princess and a magnificent feast was laid out. After all the guests had eaten and drunk as much as they wanted and danced in the great hall, the princess asked if they could all play hide-and-seek, which was a favorite game from her childhood. It was agreed

the princess should be the first to hide, and she quickly sped away.

The princess ran to a far corner of the castle and found herself climbing a spiral staircase in a turret she did not remember ever visiting before. "They will never find me here," she thought as she crept into a little room at the top. There to her surprise she found an old woman dressed in black, sitting on a chair spinning.

"What are you doing?" questioned the princess as she saw the spindle twirling, for she had never seen anything like it in her whole life.

"Come and see, pretty girl," replied the old lady. The princess watched fascinated as she pulled the strands of wool from the sheep's fleece on the floor, and twirling it deftly with her fingers fed it onto the spindle.

"Would you like to try?" she asked cunningly.

With all thoughts of hide-and-seek gone, the princess sat down and took the spindle. In a flash she pricked her thumb and even as she cried out, she fell down as though dead. The wicked fairy's spell had worked.

So did the twelfth good fairy's wish. The princess did not die, but fell into a deep deep sleep. The spell worked upon everyone else in the castle too. The king and queen slept in their chairs in the great hall. The guests dropped off to sleep as they went through the castle looking for the princess.

In the kitchen the cook fell asleep as she was about to box the pot boy's ears, and the scullery maid nodded off as she was plucking a chicken. All over the castle a great silence descended.

As the years went by a thorn hedge grew up around the castle. Passersby asked what was behind the hedge,

but few people remembered the castle where the king and queen had lived with their lovely daughter. Sometimes curious travelers tried to force their way through, but the hedge grew so thickly that they soon gave up.

One day, many many years later, a prince came by. He asked, like other travelers, what was behind the thorn hedge, which was very tall and thick by now. An old man told him a story he had heard about a castle behind the thorns, and the prince became curious. He decided to cut his way through the thorns. This time the hedge seemed to open out before his sword, and in a short while the prince was inside the grounds. He ran across the gardens and through an open door into the lovely old castle.

Everywhere he looked — in the great hall, in the kitchens, in the corridors, and on the staircases — he saw people asleep. He passed through many rooms until he found himself climbing a winding staircase in an old turret. There in a small room at the top he found himself staring in wonder at the most beautiful girl he had ever

seen. She was so lovely that without thinking he leaned forward and gently kissed her.

As his lips touched her, the princess began to stir and she opened her eyes. The first thing she saw was a handsome young man. She thought she must be dreaming, but she looked again and saw he was really there. As she gazed at him she fell in love.

They came down the turret stairs together and found the whole castle coming back to life. In the great hall the king and queen were stretching and yawning, puzzled over how they could have dropped off to sleep during their daughter's party. Their guests too were shaking their heads, rubbing their eyes, and wondering why they felt so sleepy. In the kitchen, the cook boxed the ears of the pot boy, and the scullery maid continued to pluck the chicken. Outside horses stamped and neighed in their stables, dogs barked in the yards, while in the trees birds who had stayed silent for so long burst into song. The hundred-year spell had been broken.

The princess told her parents how much she loved the handsome young man who had kissed her, and they were delighted to find he was a prince from a neighboring country. The king gave them his blessing and a grand wedding was arranged.

At the wedding party the princess looked more beautiful than ever, and the prince loved her more every moment. The twelve good fairies who had come to her Christening were invited once again and were delighted to see the happiness of the prince and princess. Toward evening the newly married pair rode off together to their new home in the prince's country, where they lived happily ever after.

GOLDILOCKS AND THE THREE BEARS

Robert Southey

Once upon a time there were three bears who lived in a house in the forest. There was a great big father bear, a middle-sized mother bear, and a tiny baby bear.

One morning, their breakfast porridge was too hot to eat, so they decided to go for a walk in the forest. While they were out, a little girl named Goldilocks came through the trees and found their house. She knocked on the door and, as there was no answer, she pushed it open and went inside.

In front of her was a table with three chairs, one large chair, one middle-sized chair, and one small chair. On the table were three bowls of porridge, one large bowl, one middle-sized bowl, and one small bowl—and three spoons.

Goldilocks was hungry and the porridge looked good, so she sat in the great big chair, picked up the large spoon and tried some of the porridge from the big bowl. But the chair was very big and very hard, the spoon was heavy, and the porridge too hot.

Goldilocks jumped off quickly and went over to the middle-sized chair. But this chair was far too soft, and when she tried the porridge from the middle-sized bowl it was too cold. So she went over to the little chair and picked up the smallest spoon and tried some of the porridge from the tiny bowl.

This time it was neither too hot nor too cold. It was just right — and so delicious that she ate it all up. But she was too heavy for the little chair and it broke in pieces under her weight.

Next Goldilocks went upstairs, where she found three beds. There was a great big bed, a middle-sized bed, and a tiny little bed. By now she was feeling tired, so she climbed into the big bed and lay down. The big bed was very hard and far too big. Then she tried the middle-sized bed, but that was far too soft, so she climbed into the tiny little bed. It was neither too hard nor too soft. In fact, it felt just right, all cosy and warm, and in no time at all Goldilocks fell fast asleep.

In a little while, the three bears came back from their walk in the forest. They saw at once that somebody had pushed open the door of their house and had been inside.

Father Bear looked around, then roared in a great big growly voice,

"SOMEBODY HAS BEEN SITTING IN MY CHAIR!"

Mother Bear said in a quiet gentle voice,

"Somebody has been sitting in my chair!"

Then Little Bear said in a small squeaky baby voice,

"Somebody has been sitting in my chair, and has broken it!"

Then Father Bear looked at his bowl of porridge and saw the spoon in it, and he said in his great big growly voice,

"SOMEBODY HAS BEEN EATING MY PORRIDGE!"

Then Mother Bear saw that her bowl had a spoon in it, and she said in her quiet gentle voice,

"Somebody has been eating my porridge!"

Little Bear looked at his porridge bowl and said in his small squeaky baby voice,

"Somebody has been eating my porridge and has eaten it all up!"

Then the three bears went upstairs, and Father Bear saw at once that his bed was messy, and he said in his

great big growly voice,

"Somebody has been sleeping in my bed!"

Mother Bear saw that her bed, too, had the bed-covers turned back, and she said in her quiet gentle voice,

"Somebody has been sleeping in my bed!"

Then Little Bear looked at his bed and said in his small squeaky baby voice,

"Somebody is sleeping in my bed, **now**!"

He squeaked so loudly that Goldilocks woke up with a start. She jumped out of bed, and away she ran, down the stairs and out into the forest. And the three bears never saw her again.

RAPUNZEL

Grimm Brothers

A long time ago, a husband and wife lived happily in a cottage at the edge of a wood. But one day the wife fell ill. She could eat nothing and grew thinner and thinner. The only thing that could cure her, she believed, was a strange herb that grew in the beautiful garden next to their cottage. She begged her husband to find a way into the garden and steal some of this herb, which was called rapunzel.

Now this garden belonged to a wicked witch, who used it to grow herbs for her spells. One day, she caught the husband creeping into her garden. When he told her what he had come for, the witch gave him some rapunzel, but she made him promise to give her their first-born child in return. The husband agreed, thinking that the witch would soon forget the promise. He took the rapunzel back to his wife, who felt better as soon as she had eaten it.

A year later, a baby girl was born, and the witch *did* come and take her away. She told the couple they would be able to see their daughter in the garden behind their house. Over the years they were able to watch her grow up into a beautiful child, with long fair hair. The witch called her Rapunzel after the plant her father had come to take.

When she was twelve years old, the witch decided to lock Rapunzel up in a high tower in case she tried to run away. The tower had no door or staircase, but Rapunzel was quite happy up there as she could sit at the window watching the life of the forest and talking to the birds. Yet sometimes she would sigh, for she longed to be back in the beautiful garden where she could run and skip in the sunshine. Then she would sing to cheer herself up.

Each day, the witch came to see her, bringing fresh food. She would stand at the bottom of the tower and call out,

"Rapunzel, Rapunzel, let down your long hair."

Rapunzel, whose long golden hair was plaited, would twist it around one of the bars and drop it out of the window, and the witch would climb up it. When she left, Rapunzel would let down her golden hair again, and the witch would slide nimbly down to the ground.

One day, the king's son was riding through the forest when he heard Rapunzel singing. Mystified, he rode to the tower, but could see no door, so could not understand how anyone could be there. He decided to stay and watch the tower and listen to the singing. After a while the witch came along and the prince watched her carefully. To his amazement, as she called out,

"Rapunzel, Rapunzel, let down your long hair," a long golden plait of hair fell almost to the ground.

The prince saw the witch climb up the hair and disappear through the window, and he made up his mind he would wait until she had gone and see if he could do the same.

So after the witch had gone, he stood where the witch had been and called,

"Rapunzel, Rapunzel, let down your long hair."

When the golden plait came tumbling down, he climbed up as the witch had done and found to his astonishment the most beautiful girl he had ever seen. They talked for a long time and then the prince left,

promising to come again. Rapunzel looked forward to his visits, for she had been lonely. He told her all about the world outside her tower, and they fell deeply in love.

One day Rapunzel said to the witch, "Why is it when you climb up my hair you are so heavy? The handsome prince who comes is much lighter than you." At this, the witch flew into a rage and took Rapunzel out of the tower and led her into the forest to a lonely spot, and told her she must stay there without food or shelter. The witch cut off Rapunzel's hair and then hurried back to the tower with the long plait of golden hair.

That evening when the prince came by, he called out as usual,

"Rapunzel, Rapunzel, let down your long hair."

The witch, who had secured the plait of golden hair inside the window, threw it down. The prince climbed up eagerly, only to be confronted with the wicked witch. "Aha," she cackled, "so you are the visitor who has been coming to see my little Rapunzel. I will make sure you won't see her again," and she tried to scratch out his eyes.

The prince jumped out of the high window, but was not killed for he landed in a clump of thorny bushes. His face, however, was badly scratched and his eyes hurt so that he could not see, and he stumbled off blindly into the forest.

After several days of wandering and suffering, he

heard a voice singing. Following the sound, he drew closer and realized he had found Rapunzel, who was singing as she worked to make a home for herself in the forest. He ran toward her, calling her name, and she came and kissed him. As she did so, his eyes were healed and he could see again.

The prince took Rapunzel to his father's palace, where he told his story. Rapunzel was reunited with her parents, who were overjoyed to see their daughter again, and a proclamation was made banning the witch from the kingdom. Then a grand wedding took place. Rapunzel married the prince and lived with him for many years. As for the witch, she was never seen again.